Maria Molina
and the Days of the Dead

by KATHLEEN KRULL • *illustrated by* ENRIQUE O. SÁNCHEZ

Macmillan Publishing Company • New York
Maxwell Macmillan Canada • Toronto
Maxwell Macmillan International • New York   Oxford   Singapore   Sydney

ACKNOWLEDGMENTS

The author would like to acknowledge the help of Gary Brewer, Barbara Fisch, Joan Mohr, and Gloria Fimbres at the University of California-San Diego, and Grace Johnson at the San Diego Museum of Man.

1 3 5 7 9 10 8 6 4 2   163020772
Library of Congress Catalog Card Number: 94-14535
ISBN 0-02-750999-0

E
KRU

For Tomie dePaola
—K. K.

To my mother
—E. O. S.

When I woke up from my nap, I was in the graveyard.

But I was not scared. Almost my whole family was there with me. Everyone except my *abuela*, my grandmother, and Pablo, my baby brother. They were buried here. My aunt and uncle were missing, too. They lived in the next village and hadn't arrived yet.

It was Pablo we were honoring that night. My brother died when he was just a few months old, not big enough to do anything besides laugh and cry and play with a few toys.

"We will honor his spirit on the first of *Los Dias de los Muertos,* 'the Days of the Dead,'" my mother told me all year. "That is the night the *angelitos,* 'the little ones,' are remembered. Perhaps Pablo will give us a sign, to let us know all is well."

In the market I had just enough money to buy one *calavera de azúcar*—a sugar-candy skull—with Pablo's name on it. Now I set it by Pablo's grave, with the other offerings.

If I lived in the United States, I, Maria Molina, would not be in a graveyard tonight. I would be out trick-or-treating on Halloween, with enough money to buy lots of candy and a fancy costume.

I drank another cup of hot chocolate and tried to stay awake. I wrapped my serape tighter around me.

My father was lighting a black beeswax candle. It lit up our offerings for Pablo—an ear of corn, his favorite toys, a piece of chocolate, many white flowers, and a small *Pan de los Muertos,* "Bread of the Dead."

"We have brought our offerings to you, Pablo," he said softly. "Come and be pleased to receive the soul of all that we have."

It wasn't much. Our family was very poor.

Suddenly the candle blew out. No one spoke at first. Was it magic? Was my brother sending us a sign? Or was it the wind?

We sat there till morning, surrounded by the sweet smell of incense, talking softly and remembering Pablo.

The next day was the second of the Days of the Dead.

"Today we honor our ancestors," my mother reminded me. "Your *abuela*."

In the morning, I helped to clean grandmother's grave and decorate it with wreaths of marigolds, the flower of the dead. We set oranges, sweet pumpkin, peanuts, and a photograph of my *abuela* on an embroidered tablecloth.

In the afternoon, I went back to our house to help my mother prepare grandmother's favorite foods—tortillas with blue corn, tamales wrapped in banana leaves, and mole, a chicken in a sauce of chocolate and chiles.

"I wish your aunt and uncle would hurry," my mother said. "They say that if you are away from home on the Days of the Dead, you might run into returning souls on the lonely roads."

"Is that really true?" I asked her, but she just smiled.

Soon my aunt and uncle *did* arrive, safely.

They took me to the market with them to buy more *Pan de los Muertos.* Bakery shelves bulged with round loaves of the special bread, glistening with reddish purple or lemon yellow glazes. Some smelled like licorice, some like cinnamon. Bakers had been working night and day for weeks, kneading, shaping, baking.

In the candy stores, piles of sugar skulls grinned at us. Bits of colored foil on fancy candies twinkled in the sun. Street vendors sold candles, bunches of fragrant herbs, wildflowers of every color, the spiciest foods and the sweetest drinks.

I held my aunt's hand tighter.

My favorite things in the market were the toys. Skeleton puppets that danced on sticks in the wind, brightly decorated masks to scare your friends with, toy coffins with skeletons that popped out when you pulled a string, skeleton earrings and necktie pins that looked like toys. Gold and silver flakes on everything, glittering in the sun.

I let go of my aunt's hand and ran to look at the tiny dolls. They had garbanzo beans for heads and little skeleton bodies, doing almost everything you can think of—taking a bath, getting married, fighting a bull, even marching in a funeral procession. My uncle bought a skeleton doll playing guitar, to set on my grandmother's grave—she had loved to play the guitar.

I had no money to buy anything, but I loved to look.

Then it was time to get back to the graveyard.

As the darkness fell, we lit candles and began keeping vigil.

My father told me what to say. "We miss you, *abuela,*" I said softly. "We have brought our offerings. Come and be pleased to receive the soul of what the land has given us."

A grasshopper flitted among the offerings. Perhaps it was magic! They say the souls of the dead inhale the tastes of their feast by way of grasshoppers or moths. Perhaps grandmother was letting us know she was pleased.

I fell asleep for a while, and when I awoke the fiesta had begun.

After a certain time, they say, the spirits of the dead go away. It is we, the living, who actually get to eat the food!

Just as the day had sparkled with colored ribbons, tissue-paper decorations, bright flowers, now the night sparkled with black-and-yellow candles and fireworks. Laughing faces loomed all around. People visited, prayed, gossiped—like a big family reunion.

I think the children had the most fun. Perhaps not as much fun as Halloween in the United States, but we were excited to be up so late, excited just to be out of school during these special days.

A group of us performed *el baile de los esqueletos,* "the dance of the skeletons," with jerky movements skeletons might make. Others told ghost stories, especially about spirits who take ghastly revenge on relatives who don't honor them properly on the Days of the Dead.

As much fun as I was having, I finally did doze off. My father had to carry me home in his arms the next morning, as we all went back to our little adobe house.

Falling asleep in my own bed, I heard my family begin planning the *next* year's celebration of *Los Dias de los Muertos*.

But by the time of the next year's Days of the Dead, something sad had happened.

No, no one else in our family had died. But my mother and father had gone North, to the United States, leaving us children with my aunt and uncle.

I missed my father and mother fiercely. Sometimes I cried.

Not long after that year's celebration in the graveyard, my parents sent word through friends that they had found a place to live. They sent word that they had found jobs, first my mother, then my father. Then they sent another kind of message.

They were coming home to fetch us children. We were *all* going to live in the United States. My aunt and uncle were coming, too. We would all be together again. We would be so much richer than we were in Mexico.

And I, Maria Molina, would celebrate Halloween now. I began thinking of costumes already, and of the mountains of sugary candy....

Still, when I came home from enjoying my first American Halloween, there was something bothering me.

"But what about Pablo? And *abuela*?" I asked my mother.

"Do you miss them?" she asked.

"We have left their spirits behind," I explained. "No one will honor them anymore on the Days of the Dead. They will be so sad."

My mother smiled. "We cannot be with them at their graves," she agreed, "but we can still honor them."

"How?" I asked.

The next night my parents showed me how.

In our apartment, we set up a small *ofrenda*, or altar. On it we placed the photograph of my grandmother, my brother's favorite toys, and a bowl of marigolds. My mother baked her own *Pan de los Muertos,* and this went on the altar, too.

All night we kept vigil. Before I fell asleep, I looked all around at my family.

And it *was* magic, the most magic thing of all.

STORYTELLER'S NOTE

Sugar skulls, graveside picnics, and "Bread of the Dead" may seem weird and ghoulish to North Americans.

But in Mexico, the Days of the Dead (*Los Días de los Muertos*) are a hopeful time when the living and dead are united in a celebration of family history. October 31 and November 1 and 2 are some of the most important days of the year—national holidays as well as a religious fiesta. They combine Spanish Roman Catholic ritual and ancient Indian beliefs. The concept of death is not kept hidden away, but introduced at a very early age.

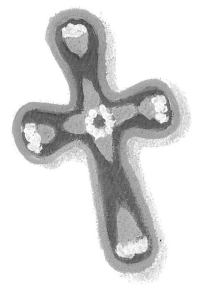

Customs differ from village to village. Most celebrations include visits to cemeteries for cleaning and decorating the graves of the dead. The atmosphere is festive, not weepy or scary. If the right rituals are followed, the spirits of lost loved ones are thought to partake of what has been prepared for them. It's widely believed that the dead guide the living, delivering advice and even punishment when necessary.

Gifts for the dead include candles, incense, flowers, and the richest foods—the dead don't actually eat the food, but inhale its essence. The offerings are elaborate or simple, depending on the financial condition of the family that year. But if *nothing* is offered, revenge can be wreaked by ghosts on stingy or unbelieving relatives. The presence of the dead can be symbolized by a moth or by slight signals—a candle flickering, a glass tipping over.

Necessary to each family's celebration is a gaily decorated, cakelike bread called *Pan de los Muertos*, or "Bread of the Dead." Every baker in the market stocks up on this anise-flavored bread, which is made only at this time of year. It is oval-shaped to represent the imagined souls of the dead, or sometimes shaped like animals or people. It can be decorated with angel faces, or with little knobs of dough to represent the bones of the dead or the tears of the living.

In the markets you can also buy handmade sugar skulls, or *calaveras*, and grinning skeletons miming all sorts of human activity. The display is amusing and joyful rather than gruesome. In Mexican tradition, death is accepted bravely and even with humor, in the belief that death and life are part of the same cycle.

FOR FURTHER READING

Ancona, George. *Pablo Remembers: The Fiesta of the Day of the Dead*. New York: Lothrop, 1993.

Greenleigh, John. *The Days of the Dead: Mexico's Festival of Communion with the Departed*. San Francisco: Collins Publishers, 1991.

Shalant, Phyllis. *Look What We've Brought You from Mexico: Crafts, Games, Recipes, Stories and Other Cultural Activities from Mexican-Americans*. New York: Julian Messner, 1992.

Westridge Young Writers Workshop. *Kids Explore America's Hispanic Heritage*. Santa Fe: John Muir, 1992.

Step-by-Step Recipe for
Pan de los Muertos, "Bread of the Dead"

1. Ask an adult to help you. Preheat the oven to 400 degrees.

2. Grease a large cookie sheet.

3. Mix the following ingredients in a large bowl until smooth:
   2 cups all-purpose flour
   2 teaspoons baking powder
   2 tablespoons sugar
   ¼ teaspoon salt
   1 egg
   ⅔ cup milk
   ¼ cup vegetable oil
   10 drops anise extract (a flavoring something like licorice)

4. With clean hands, either mold the dough into one large round shape with a raised knob in the middle, or break the dough into smaller amounts and make many round shapes. You can also mold the dough into the shapes of animals, faces, or angels. Place the dough on the cookie sheet.

5. In a smaller bowl, mix these ingredients for the topping:
   ¼ cup brown sugar
   1 tablespoon all-purpose flour
   1 teaspoon ground cinnamon
   1 tablespoon melted butter

6. Sprinkle the topping on the dough.

7. Bake for 20 to 25 minutes.

8. Serve warm with milk.